THE BLOOMING DESTINY OF JASTYN

Kenneth Haines
The Blooming Destiny of Jastyn

Published by Spines Publishing Platform
ISBN: 979-8-89691-740-3

THE BLOOMING DESTINY OF JASTYN

KENNETH HAINES

CONTENTS

CHAPTER ONE

THE WHISPERING PETALS

THE BIRTH OF JASTYN

In the heart of the Eternal Garden, where the air was thick with the fragrance of blooming flowers, Jastyn made her entrance into the world. The moment she took her first breath, her surroundings seemed to pulse with life, as if the very essence of the garden acknowledged her presence. Each petal that unfurled around her whispered secrets of ancient times, while the vibrant colors danced in harmony with the gentle breeze. Jastyn was born not just into a realm of beauty but into a legacy steeped in magic and purpose, where each bloom was a testament to the stories and memories of those who had come before.

From her earliest days, Jastyn was enveloped in the warmth of the Eternal Garden, nurtured by the elemental forces that governed this mystical land. The Elders, wise beings who had watched over the garden for centuries, recognized her as a child of destiny. Yet, in her innocence, Jastyn remained oblivious to the weight of her significance. She spent her days weaving garlands of flowers, laughing with the woodland creatures, and playing beneath the shade of towering trees that had witnessed the ages. The garden was her playground, a sanctuary of untainted joy and wonder, shielding her from the encroaching darkness that would one day threaten their existence.

As Jastyn grew, the radiant beauty of the garden began to dim. Shadows crept along the pathways, and the once-vibrant blooms started to wilt. The

Elders sensed the shift in the balance of their realm, as a malevolent force sought to drain the life from the sacred flowers. Jastyn, too, felt the change; a heaviness settled in her heart, and the laughter of her youth became tinged with an unshakable sense of foreboding. It was during one of these somber moments that she overheard the Elders whispering about the prophecy tied to her name, a prophecy that spoke of a chosen one who would rise to restore the light.

The revelation of her destiny struck Jastyn like a bolt of lightning, illuminating the depths of her soul. The gift she had been given was more than mere existence; it was a call to action. With newfound resolve, she began to explore the depths of the garden, seeking the wisdom of the ancient flowers and the hidden powers that lay within them. Each encounter revealed fragments of her purpose, connecting her to the rich tapestry of life that surrounded her. The realization that she was the Gift from God filled her with both dread and exhilaration, as she understood that she alone held the key to the garden's salvation.

In the face of encroaching darkness, Jastyn emerged as a beacon of hope. The journey ahead would challenge her in ways she could scarcely imagine, testing her courage and the purity of her heart. Yet, she was not alone. The spirits of the garden, intertwined with her fate, began to guide her, revealing the path she must take to reclaim the Eternal Garden. The birth of Jastyn marked not just the beginning of a life but the awakening of a powerful force destined to confront the shadows and usher in a new era of blooming beauty and eternal light.

THE MYSTICAL REALM OF FLORA

In the mystical realm of Flora, the landscape is a vibrant tapestry woven with countless varieties of flowers, each more enchanting than the last. This extraordinary world is not merely an array of colors and fragrances but a complex ecosystem where every bloom serves as a vessel of ancient power. The flora of this realm possesses a deep connection to the energies of the universe, drawing upon the life force that permeates the air. Each flower tells a story, whispering secrets to those who are attuned to its essence. From the delicate petals of the Moonlit Orchid to the towering stems of the Celestial Sunflower, every species plays a crucial role in maintaining the balance of life in Flora.

Jastyn, the protagonist of this unfolding tale, grows up amidst the lush beauty of this mystical realm, initially oblivious to the profound significance of the flowers surrounding her. Raised by wise and nurturing guardians, she learns to appreciate the aesthetics of her environment but remains unaware of her extraordinary destiny. The Elders of the Eternal Garden, ancient beings tasked with safeguarding the realm's magical heritage, have chosen her for a purpose that transcends her understanding. These Elders, attuned to the rhythms of life, recognize the purity in Jastyn's heart and the latent power within her, marking her as a beacon of hope for Flora.

As shadows begin to encroach upon the vibrant landscape, a malevolent force threatens to drain the life essence from the sacred flowers. This darkness, a harbinger of despair, seeks to disrupt the harmony that has thrived for centuries. The flowers, once thriving with vitality, begin to wither, their colors fading, and their fragrances dulled. This alarming shift draws the attention of Jastyn, awakening her dormant connection to the flora around her. With each wilting petal and fading bloom, she feels a stirring within, a call to action that compels her to uncover the truth behind her existence and the prophecy entwined with her name.

As Jastyn ventures deeper into the heart of Flora, she encounters allies and mentors who guide her on her journey. They reveal the ancient lore of the realm, explaining how each flower is a guardian of memories, carrying echoes of the past that can be harnessed for healing and restoration. Here, she learns that her role is not merely to observe but to actively participate in the realm's revival. The Elders impart wisdom that emphasizes the importance of unity with nature, teaching her that the strength of the flowers lies in their interconnectedness. Jastyn begins to understand that her journey is one of self-discovery, leading her to embrace her identity as the Gift from God.

Through her trials and tribulations, Jastyn becomes a symbol of hope, embodying the resilience and beauty of the mystical realm of Flora. As she confronts the darkness threatening her world, she draws upon the stories and memories encapsulated in each flower, using their power to reclaim what has been lost. Her evolution from a sheltered girl to a fierce protector of the Eternal Garden illustrates the profound bond between humanity and nature. In the end, Jastyn's journey reveals that the true essence of the mystical realm of Flora lies not just in the beauty of its blooms but in the strength and courage of those who dare to protect it.

THE ELDERS' WATCHFUL EYES

The Elders of the Eternal Garden are ancient beings, guardians of the mystical realm that cradles Jastyn's destiny. They embody wisdom gathered over millennia, their presence felt in the gentle rustle of leaves and the vibrant colors of blooms. Each Elder represents a different aspect of nature—growth, healing, wisdom, and balance. They are not merely observers; their watchful eyes monitor the pulse of the garden, ensuring that the delicate equilibrium between light and dark remains intact. As the protectors of the sacred land, they possess the ability to commune with the flowers, drawing forth their memories and understanding the whispers of the earth.

Jastyn, in her early years, remains blissfully unaware of the Elders and their significance. She plays among the flowers, her laughter ringing like a melody through the petals. However, the Elders have always been aware of her presence, recognizing the purity of her heart and the unique energy that emanates from her very being. They have seen the potential within her, a potential intertwined with the fate of the garden itself. Jastyn's joyful interactions with the flora ignite a flicker of hope in the Elders, who know that her destiny is tied to the ancient prophecy that has been foretold.

As darkness encroaches upon the realm, the Elders' watchful eyes grow heavier with concern. The once-vibrant blooms begin to wilt, their colors dimming as if the very essence of life is being siphoned away. The Elders gather in a sacred circle, their ethereal forms shimmering with urgency. They share their visions of the impending doom, realizing that the time has come to reveal the truth to Jastyn. The darkness is not merely a physical threat; it is a manifestation of despair and disconnection from nature's harmony, and only Jastyn can rekindle the light.

In a moment of revelation, the Elders choose to unveil their existence to Jastyn. They appear to her in a luminous haze, their voices intertwining like a gentle breeze. They bestow upon her the knowledge of her lineage and the prophecy that binds her to the garden. Jastyn learns that she is not just a child of the realm but the chosen one destined to restore balance and heal the withering flowers. The weight of this knowledge is both exhilarating and daunting, as she grapples with the enormity of her responsibility.

With the Elders' guidance, Jastyn begins her journey of understanding and empowerment. They teach her the language of the flowers, how to listen to their stories, and how to harness the ancient power that resides within her. Through their watchful eyes, she learns the importance of nurturing not only the garden but also the connections between herself and all living beings. As she steps into her role as the bearer of the Gift of the Eternal Bloom, the Elders stand steadfastly by her side, ready to support her as she faces the darkness that threatens her world.

CHAPTER TWO

THE ETERNAL GARDEN

THE LEGENDS OF THE GARDEN

The legends of the Garden are woven into the very fabric of Jastyn's existence, echoing through the whispers of the wind and the rustling of leaves. According to ancient texts, the Eternal Garden was created by the Elders, mystical beings who understood the balance of nature and the significance of every bloom. Each flower in this enchanted realm serves a dual purpose, acting as both a source of beauty and a keeper of stories from generations past. These legends have been passed down through oral traditions, often recounted by those who have ventured close to the Garden, creating a tapestry of narratives that illustrate the deep connection between the flowers and the beings who inhabit this world.

One of the most prominent legends speaks of the first bloom, known as the Celestial Blossom. This flower is said to have emerged at the dawn of creation, imbued with the essence of life itself. It is believed that the Celestial Blossom is the progenitor of all flowers in the Garden, each carrying a fragment of its original power. When the Celestial Blossom flourished, it brought harmony to the realm, allowing the Elders to cultivate a sanctuary where both nature and magic thrived. The legend of this flower serves as a reminder of the potential that lies within every bloom, hinting at the interconnectedness of life and the crucial role that Jastyn must play in restoring balance to the Garden.

As Jastyn grows, she learns of another legend concerning the Bloom of

Echoes, a flower that captures the memories of those who have walked the paths of the Garden. It is said that the Bloom of Echoes can reveal the truth behind one's destiny and illuminate the choices that led them to their current path. This flower holds a special significance for Jastyn, as it is believed that her journey will require her to confront the past and understand the sacrifices made by those who came before her. Through the stories embedded within the Bloom of Echoes, Jastyn will unearth the layers of her own identity and the legacy that has shaped her purpose.

The legends also warn of the Shadow Blight, an ominous force that has begun to consume the once-vibrant flowers of the Garden. As darkness creeps into this sacred space, the stories of hope and resilience become crucial for the inhabitants of the realm. The Elders tell of a prophecy that speaks of a chosen one—an individual destined to face the encroaching darkness and restore the light to the Garden. This prophecy resonates deeply with Jastyn, as she starts to uncover her connection to the legends and recognizes that her name itself is intertwined with the fate of the blooms. Her journey through the Garden will not only be one of self-discovery but also a battle against the forces that threaten to extinguish the very essence of life.

Ultimately, the legends of the Garden serve as a guiding light for Jastyn as she navigates her path in a world fraught with challenges. They remind her that every flower, every story, and every choice carries weight and significance. As she embraces her role as the Gift from God, Jastyn's understanding of the legends and their meanings will empower her to harness the ancient powers that dwell within the blooms. In doing so, she will not only reclaim the lost vitality of the Eternal Garden but also fulfill the prophecy that has awaited her arrival. The legends are not just tales of the past; they are the keys to unlocking a future filled with hope, resilience, and the eternal bloom of life.

THE SIGNIFICANCE OF THE BLOOMS

The blooms in Jastyn's realm serve as more than mere decorations of nature; they are integral to the balance of life and magic. Each flower represents a unique facet of existence, embodying stories and emotions that transcend time. From the vibrant petals of the Sunflower of Joy to the delicate Whispering Violets that carry secrets, every bloom holds significance. These flowers are the lifeblood of the mystical world, connecting its inhabitants to the ancient energies that sustain their lives. As Jastyn navigates her journey, she begins to understand that the blooms are not just passive objects but active participants in the narrative of her destiny.

The Elders of the Eternal Garden, custodians of this mystical realm, recognize the power embedded within each flower. They believe that the blooms are manifestations of collective memories and experiences, serving as living libraries of the past. This connection is particularly profound in Jastyn's case, as her very existence is intertwined with the blooms' essence. As she grows and learns, the stories of the flowers begin to reveal themselves to her, offering guidance and insight into her role within the larger tapestry of life. The significance of the blooms becomes increasingly apparent as they guide her through adversity, helping her to unlock her potential.

However, the encroaching darkness threatens not only the physical beauty of the flowers but also the very foundation of the realm's magic. As the life force of the sacred blooms is siphoned away, the vibrant colors fade, and the stories they carry risk being forgotten. Jastyn's awakening to her destiny is marked by a deepening understanding of this crisis. The blooms symbolize hope, resilience, and the interconnectedness of all living things. They remind her that the fight against darkness is not merely a battle for survival but a quest to preserve the essence of life itself.

Moreover, the blooms serve as a reflection of Jastyn's internal journey. Each flower she encounters mirrors her emotional state and personal growth. The once-ignorant girl begins to blossom into a powerful force of nature, echoing the transformation of the blooms around her. This parallel serves to illustrate how her character development is inextricably linked to the fate of the flowers. As she embraces her role as the Gift from God, Jastyn learns that nurturing the blooms is synonymous with nurturing her own spirit. The act of tending to the flowers becomes a metaphor for self-discovery and empowerment, reinforcing the idea that the care we give to the world around us reflects the care we must also give to ourselves.

In conclusion, the significance of the blooms in "The Blooming Destiny of Jastyn" extends far beyond their aesthetic appeal. They are vessels of ancient wisdom, symbols of hope, and reflections of personal growth. As Jastyn embarks on her journey to confront the darkness, the blooms become her allies, each one whispering secrets of strength and resilience. Through their stories, she learns that her destiny is not only to protect the sacred flowers but also to embrace the power of her own bloom. In this intricate dance of life and magic, the blooms are a testament to the enduring spirit of existence, reminding us all of the beauty and significance of our own journeys.

JASTYN'S FIRST ENCOUNTER

Jastyn's journey began in the heart of the Eternal Garden, a realm where colors danced in vibrant hues and fragrances whispered secrets of ages past. As she wandered among the towering blooms, each petal seemed to hum with energy, resonating with the life force that pulsed through the ground. The flowers were not mere plants; they were sentinels of ancient power, guardians of wisdom that had been nurtured through generations. Jastyn, with her innocence and curiosity, often spent hours lost in their beauty, unaware of the profound connection she shared with these mystical entities.

On the eve of her sixteenth birthday, a peculiar event unfolded. As twilight draped the garden in a soft glow, Jastyn stumbled upon a flower she had never seen before. It stood apart from the others, its petals shimmering with an other-worldly light, pulsating gently as if it had a heartbeat of its own. Drawn to it like a moth to a flame, she reached out, and the moment her fingers brushed against the delicate petals, a surge of energy coursed through her. Visions flooded her mind—images of a time long forgotten, filled with joy, sorrow, and the promise of a destiny waiting to be fulfilled.

In that instant, Jastyn felt a connection deeper than she had ever known. The flower, a rare and sacred bloom known as the Lumina Blossom, was said to be the embodiment of hope and renewal. It whispered tales of the Elders, ancient beings entrusted with the protection of the Eternal Garden. They had chosen her, not by coincidence, but by design, as the one destined to restore balance to the realm now threatened by encroaching darkness. With each vision, she understood that her existence was intertwined with the fate of the garden and the life force of all its flowers.

As the night deepened, Jastyn's heart raced with both excitement and trepi-dation. The Lumina Blossom revealed the first steps of her journey—a quest to awaken the dormant energies of the garden and to confront the darkness that sought to consume it. With this newfound knowledge, she felt a weight of responsibility settle upon her shoulders. Yet, alongside that weight, there was an exhilarating sense of purpose. She was meant for more than the ordinary life she had led; she was a vessel of change, a beacon of hope in a world teetering on the brink of despair.

With dawn approaching, Jastyn made her way back through the garden, her heart brimming with determination. The air was thick with the scent of awakening blooms, and she could feel the pulse of the Eternal Garden synchronizing with her own. She understood now that her first encounter with the Lumina Blossom was just the beginning. It was a call to action, a reminder that she was not alone in this fight. The Elders were watching, the flowers were waiting, and the destiny of the garden rested in her hands. Jastyn took a deep breath, embracing the path ahead, ready to bloom into the role she was destined to fulfill.

CHAPTER THREE
AWAKENING THE GIFT

THE CALL OF THE BLOSSOMS

In the realm of Jastyn, the arrival of spring heralds more than just a change in seasons; it marks the awakening of the blossoms that serve as the lifeblood of the land. Each flower in this mystical world is imbued with ancient power, a connection to the past, and a promise for the future. The vibrant colors and intoxicating scents are not mere aesthetic pleasures but are tied to the very essence of existence itself. The Elders of the Eternal Garden, guardians of this sacred realm, have long known that the vitality of their world hinges upon the flowers, each representing a unique story and a vital purpose within the grand tapestry of life.

Jastyn, unaware of her destiny, has always been drawn to the blooms that surround her. From a young age, she played among the fields, her laughter intertwined with the whispers of petals swaying in the breeze. The Elders watched over her, recognizing the purity of her heart and the potential that lay dormant within her spirit. However, as the shadows of darkness began to creep into the vibrant landscape, the connection between Jastyn and the blossoms became crucial. The flowers started to wilt, their colors fading as a malevolent force sought to drain the life from the Eternal Garden.

As she explored the gardens, Jastyn began to notice the subtle changes in her surroundings. The once-lush greenery was now marred by patches of decay, and the air that was once fragrant with floral notes grew heavy with a sense of foreboding. In her heart, she felt a stirring, an inexplicable call that urged her to seek out the source of the darkness. It was as if the blossoms themselves were reaching out to her, their silent cries for help resonating within her very being. This call was the first step on her journey, leading her to uncover the truth about her heritage and the prophecy that entwined her fate with the fate of the flowers.

The significance of her name, Jastyn, began to unravel before her. Each letter echoed the ancient tales told by the Elders, stories filled with valor, sacrifice, and the triumph of light over darkness. As she delved deeper into the lore of her ancestors, Jastyn realized that she was not merely a bystander in this unfolding drama; she was the key to reviving the blooms and restoring balance to her world. Her heart surged with newfound determination as she embraced her role as the Gift from God, destined to protect the Eternal Garden from the encroaching shadows.

The call of the blossoms was not just a summons for help; it was a call to action. Jastyn understood that to answer this call, she would need to harness the ancient powers entwined within each flower, learning to communicate with them and understand their stories. As she took her first steps into this uncharted territory, the weight of her responsibility pressed upon her, yet the vibrant colors of the blooms surrounding her sparked courage within her soul. In the heart of the garden, where life and death intertwined, Jastyn would forge her path, guided by the whispers of the blossoms and the light of hope that flickered within her.

DISCOVERING HIDDEN POWERS

In the mystical realm of Jastyn, flowers are more than mere flora; they embody ancient powers that shape the very essence of life. Each blossom holds the whispers of history, weaving tales of joy, sorrow, and the interconnectedness of all beings. This sacred bond between the flora and the land is not merely a coincidence but a reflection of the deeper magic that pulses through the Eternal Garden. As Jastyn traverses her world, she begins to notice the subtle changes around her—the wilting petals, the dimming colors, and the growing shadows that encroach upon the vibrancy of her surroundings. These signs herald a shift, one that compels her to delve deeper into her identity and the untapped potential within her.

The Elders of the Eternal Garden, guardians of this enchanted realm, have long awaited the arrival of a chosen one. Unbeknownst to Jastyn, her very name is steeped in prophecy, a beacon of hope destined to illuminate the darkness threatening to engulf their world. The hidden powers she possesses are intricately linked to the flowers themselves, each bloom resonating with a unique energy that she must learn to harness. With every step she takes, Jastyn begins to unravel the tapestry of her lineage, discovering that her connection to the flowers is not merely a passive bond but a profound responsibility that she must embrace.

As Jastyn embarks on her journey of self-discovery, she encounters challenges that test her resolve and courage. The encroaching darkness manifests in various forms—twisted vines that choke the life out of the soil, creatures born from despair, and illusions that threaten to mislead her. Each trial serves to awaken the dormant powers within her, forcing Jastyn to confront her fears and insecurities. In these moments of struggle, she learns to listen to the ancient songs of the flowers, understanding that they hold the keys to her awakening. Through perseverance and introspection, she begins to cultivate her gifts, allowing the essence of the blooms to guide her path.

The turning point arrives when Jastyn discovers a hidden grove, a sanctuary untouched by the dark forces. Here, the flowers bloom in radiant hues, vibrant and alive, resonating with a powerful energy that invigorates her spirit. It is within this sacred space that she encounters the spirits of the flowers, ethereal beings who reveal the true nature of her powers. They impart wisdom, teaching her how to channel the energy of the blooms to combat the darkness. Jastyn realizes that her abilities are not solely for her own benefit; they are meant to restore the balance of life and protect the realm she holds dear. This revelation ignites a sense of purpose within her, transforming her fear into determination.

Armed with newfound knowledge and strength, Jastyn emerges from the hidden grove ready to confront the encroaching shadows. The journey ahead will not be easy, but she is no longer the unaware girl she once was. With the support of the flowers and the guidance of the Elders, Jastyn embraces her role as the Gift from God, a vessel through which the ancient powers of the Eternal Garden will flourish anew. As she steps into her destiny, she understands that true power lies not just in the abilities she possesses, but in her unwavering commitment to protect the beauty and life that the flowers represent. The unfolding chapters of her journey will reveal not only the depth of her powers but also the strength of her heart in the face of adversity.

THE PROPHECY REVEALED

The prophecy revealed itself in whispers carried by the winds of the Eternal Garden, a place untouched by time yet deeply intertwined with the fate of the realm. Jastyn, a child of the blooming flowers, had always felt a connection to them, but it was only as she turned thirteen that the true significance of her bond began to unfold. The Elders, ancient beings who safeguarded the garden's secrets, sensed the encroaching darkness that threatened their world. As the light within the flowers dimmed, they gathered to unveil the prophecy that had long been shrouded in mystery, a prophecy that spoke of a girl destined to restore balance and vitality to the realm.

In the heart of the garden, beneath the towering blossoms that swayed gently in the breeze, the Elders convened. They revealed to Jastyn that her name was not merely a label but a beacon of hope. "Jastyn," they chanted in unison, "the Blooming Destiny is intertwined with your spirit." The words echoed through the air, resonating with the very essence of the flowers around her. Each petal seemed to shimmer with an understanding, a recognition of the weight her name carried. Jastyn listened intently, her heart racing as the Elders recounted the tale of an ancient curse that had begun to awaken, one that sought to drain the life from the garden and plunge the world into eternal darkness.

As the Elders spoke, Jastyn learned that she was born under a rare celestial alignment, a cosmic event that only occurred once every millennium. This alignment had marked her as the chosen one, destined to wield the powers of the Eternal Bloom. The prophecy foretold of her journey through trials that would test her strength, courage, and purity of heart. Only by embracing her true nature could she harness the ancient magic of the flowers and wield it against the encroaching darkness. With every word, Jastyn felt the weight of her destiny pressing upon her, but alongside it blossomed a sense of determination.

The Elders imparted to Jastyn the sacred knowledge of the flowers—their healing properties, their stories, and the memories they held. Each bloom was a fragment of the past, a reminder of the love, joy, and sorrow that had shaped the garden. As Jastyn listened, she understood that her connection to these flowers was not just personal; it was integral to the fabric of the realm itself. The more she learned, the more she felt the call of the flowers, urging her to awaken the dormant powers within herself and to prepare for the journey that lay ahead.

With the prophecy now revealed, Jastyn stood on the precipice of her destiny. The Elders entrusted her with a sacred task: to venture beyond the garden's borders and confront the source of the darkness. Armed with the knowledge of her heritage and the strength of the blooms, she was ready to embark on a quest that would not only define her existence but also determine the fate of the Eternal Garden. As the first rays of dawn illuminated the flowers around her, Jastyn took a deep breath, feeling the pulse of the garden within her. The journey was about to begin, and with it, the chance to awaken the world to its true, vibrant potential.

CHAPTER FOUR

SHADOWS OVER THE LAND

THE ARRIVAL OF DARKNESS

The arrival of darkness in the realm of Jastyn marked a pivotal moment in the balance of nature and magic. This darkness was not an ordinary nightfall; it was a creeping shadow that siphoned vitality from the vibrant blooms that adorned the Eternal Garden. As the sun dipped below the horizon, an unsettling chill settled over the land, causing the flowers to wilt and their colors to fade. The Elders of the Eternal Garden, wise and ancient beings, sensed the encroaching threat. They gathered in solemn assembly, their faces etched with concern, as they deliberated on the means to confront this malevolent force.

As the darkness spread, it became evident that it was more than just a physical blight. It was a manifestation of despair and malice, rooted deeply in the hearts of those who had forgotten the sacred bond with nature. The once harmonious melodies of the garden were replaced by an eerie silence, leaving Jastyn and the inhabitants of the realm in a state of dread. The Elders, seeing the impact of this darkness, recognized that it was a test of resilience and purity of heart. They understood that Jastyn, though still unaware of her destiny, was central to restoring the balance that had been disrupted.

Jastyn, who had spent her childhood playing amidst the flowers, began to notice their distress. The petals that once danced in the gentle breeze now drooped, their once-lively scents dulled by the pervasive gloom. Driven by an instinct she could not quite articulate, she ventured deeper into the heart of the garden, where the most sacred blooms resided. It was there that she encountered the first signs of the ancient power that coursed through her veins, igniting a flicker of hope in her spirit. The Elders, observing her journey, recognized the spark within her—a potential that must be nurtured to combat the encroaching darkness.

As the shadows deepened, the Elders revealed to Jastyn the truth of her lineage and the prophecy that surrounded her name. She was the chosen one, a beacon of light destined to wield the gift of the Eternal Bloom. This revelation was both a burden and a blessing; Jastyn felt the weight of expectation settle upon her shoulders. Yet, it also ignited a fierce determination within her. She understood that the fate of the garden and its ancient magic rested in her hands. The darkness could not be allowed to extinguish the vibrant life force that was so integral to the realm.

With newfound purpose, Jastyn began her quest to confront the darkness. She sought guidance from the Elders, who imparted their wisdom and shared the sacred rituals of the garden. Armed with knowledge and the love of the blooms that surrounded her, Jastyn set forth to restore the light that had been dimmed. The journey ahead would be fraught with challenges, but she was resolute in her mission. As she stepped into the unknown, the resilience of her spirit mirrored the tenacity of the flowers that had thrived for centuries. In this battle against the darkness, Jastyn would not only discover her true self but also reignite the eternal bond between her world and the sacred blooms that defined it.

THE WITHERING OF THE FLOWERS

In the realm of Jastyn, the vibrancy of life was closely intertwined with the flowers that adorned the landscape. Each blossom was not merely a visual delight; it embodied the essence of the ancient powers that governed the balance of nature. The flowers whispered secrets of the past, their petals unfurling stories that resonated with the heartbeat of the earth. However, as darkness began to encroach upon this mystical land, the once-lush gardens began to exhibit signs of distress. The vibrant colors faded, and the sweet fragrances that once filled the air turned stale, signaling a deeper malaise that threatened the very fabric of Jastyn's existence.

The Elders of the Eternal Garden, guardians of the sacred flora, sensed the impending doom. Their ancient wisdom indicated that the withering of the flowers was not merely a natural occurrence but a manifestation of a greater evil seeking to siphon the life force from the realm. As the flowers drooped and wilted, they became shadows of their former selves, stripped of the stories they once held. The elders convened in solemn gatherings, their faces etched with worry, recognizing that the fate of Jastyn rested in the hands of one destined to restore the balance—a task that would require courage, sacrifice, and an unwavering belief in the power of hope.

Jastyn, blissfully unaware of her significance, roamed the gardens with a childlike wonder, oblivious to the changes taking place around her. The flowers that once reached for the sky now huddled close to the ground, their vibrant hues dimmed to muted pastels. It was during these moments of quiet reflection that Jastyn began to feel a connection to the very essence of the flowers. She sensed their pain, their longing for the sunlight and warmth that had become scarce. This connection sparked a flicker of determination within her, igniting a desire to uncover the truth behind the fading blooms and the darkness that loomed over her homeland.

As Jastyn ventured deeper into the mysteries of the Eternal Garden, she stumbled upon forgotten prophecies etched in the bark of ancient trees. The words spoke of a chosen one, a figure who would rise to combat the encroaching shadows and restore the flowers to their former glory. The realization that her name was intertwined with these prophecies sent shivers down her spine, awakening a sense of purpose she had never known. The withering of the flowers was not just an environmental crisis; it was a call to action, urging her to embrace her destiny and harness the power that lay dormant within her.

With each step she took, Jastyn felt the weight of her lineage and the responsibility that came with it. The withering flowers were a reflection of the struggles that lay ahead, but they also represented the potential for rebirth and renewal. She understood that her journey would not be easy, yet she was determined to confront the darkness and restore the eternal bloom to her beloved realm. The petals that had fallen to the ground were not merely remnants of a bygone era; they were seeds of hope, waiting for the right moment to take root once more. Through her unwavering resolve, Jastyn would become the catalyst for healing, breathing life back into the flowers and, in turn, reviving the spirit of Jastyn itself.

THE ELDERS' DESPERATION

The Elders of the Eternal Garden, guardians of the mystical realm, found themselves in a state of growing despair. For centuries, they had nurtured the sacred flowers that symbolized life, hope, and the wisdom of ages. Each bloom not only served as a vessel of ancient power but also as a connection to the very essence of their world. However, as darkness began to seep into the land, the Elders witnessed the vibrant colors of their cherished flowers fading, replaced by a pallor that signaled impending doom. Their once harmonious existence was now threatened, and the urgency to protect their sacred realm became a consuming desperation.

The Elders convened in the heart of the Eternal Garden, where the most ancient and revered blooms stood as witnesses to their plight. They exchanged anxious glances, each aware that the time for action had come. They recalled the prophecies whispered by the winds, tales of a chosen one destined to restore balance and light. Jastyn, a child unaware of her significance, was the embodiment of that prophecy. The Elders had watched over her since her birth, waiting for the moment when she would awaken to her true potential. Yet, as the darkness encroached, their hope began to wane, and the burden of their responsibility weighed heavily upon them.

In their desperation, the Elders sought guidance from the oldest and wisest flower, the Lumina Blossom. For generations, this bloom had served as a beacon of light and wisdom, its petals shimmering with ethereal energy. The Elders gathered around it and invoked the ancient rites, praying for clarity and a renewed sense of purpose. Through the gentle rustling of its petals, they felt a surge of energy that spoke to them in soft whispers, urging them to act swiftly. The Lumina Blossom revealed that Jastyn was not merely a child but a vital link between the realms of light and shadow. It was her destiny to confront the darkness that threatened to consume their world.

Recognizing the gravity of their mission, the Elders made a pact to guide Jastyn on her journey. They devised a plan to reveal her true nature and the power she possessed. Each Elder took it upon themselves to impart their wisdom and share the stories of the blooms, ensuring that Jastyn would understand the significance of her role. They knew that awakening her potential would require more than just knowledge; it would demand courage and resilience in the face of overwhelming odds. As the darkness continued to spread, the Elders felt a flicker of hope igniting within them, fueled by the belief that Jastyn could be the light they so desperately needed.

With their hearts set on the path ahead, the Elders prepared to summon Jastyn to the heart of the Eternal Garden, where the Lumina Blossom awaited her presence. They understood that the time had come to unveil the truth of her existence, to share with her the burden and the honor of her calling. As they looked upon the wilting flowers, a sense of urgency gripped them; they could not afford to delay. The fate of their realm hung in the balance, and they were determined to arm Jastyn with the knowledge and strength needed to combat the encroaching darkness. The Elders' desperation transformed into resolve, and they braced themselves for the moment that would change everything.

CHAPTER FIVE
THE JOURNEY BEGINS

ALLIES IN THE GARDEN

In the mystical realm of Jastyn, the connections between nature and its inhabitants run deeper than mere existence; they are interwoven with magic and ancient wisdom. The concept of allies in the garden extends beyond companionship; it embodies the intricate relationships between Jastyn and the sentient flowers that thrive in the Eternal Garden. Each bloom, with its vibrant colors and unique fragrances, serves as a guardian, protector, and guide in Jastyn's journey. These flowers, imbued with the power of the Elders, are not passive entities but active participants in the unfolding narrative of the realm, providing wisdom and assistance as Jastyn faces the encroaching darkness.

As Jastyn begins to understand her role in the fight against the malevolent forces threatening the Eternal Garden, she learns that her allies are not merely plants but embodiments of elemental forces. The Rose of Resilience, for instance, teaches her about strength in adversity, while the Lily of Purity symbolizes clarity of purpose. Each flower shares its essence with Jastyn, enhancing her abilities and deepening her connection to the garden. Through their interactions, she gains insights into the history of her world and the significance of her destiny, transforming her from a naive girl into a determined protector of the realm.

The bond between Jastyn and her floral allies is further strengthened by the trials they face together. As darkness spreads, the flowers begin to wilt, their colors fading, and their energies diminishing. This physical manifestation of the threat galvanizes Jastyn into action. She learns to harness the unique powers of each flower, combining their strengths to create powerful spells that can repel the shadow creeping into their world. The act of nurturing these flowers not only revitalizes them but also reinforces her own innate abilities, allowing her to grow alongside her allies in a symbiotic relationship that is crucial to her development.

Jastyn's journey is also marked by moments of self-discovery facilitated by her floral companions. The garden becomes a sanctuary where she confronts her fears and doubts. The Sunflower of Courage encourages her to face the darkness head-on, while the Orchid of Wisdom reminds her that patience and understanding are paramount in overcoming obstacles. Each interaction reveals hidden facets of her character, helping her to embrace her identity as the chosen one. This internal growth parallels the external struggle, emphasizing the importance of harmony between the inner self and the outer world.

Ultimately, "Allies in the Garden" illustrates that the fight against darkness is not a solitary endeavor. Jastyn's relationships with her floral allies serve as a reminder of the interconnectedness of all living beings in the mystical realm. As the story unfolds, it becomes clear that the true power lies not just in individual strength but in unity and collaboration. Together, Jastyn and her allies symbolize hope, resilience, and the eternal bloom of life, embodying the essence of the prophecy that binds them to their fate. The garden, with its vibrant blooms and ancient magic, becomes a living testament to the enduring spirit of friendship and the transformative power of working together against adversity.

TRIALS AND TRIBULATIONS

Trials and tribulations are inevitable in the life of Jastyn, a young girl destined to protect the sacred balance of her mystical realm. From an early age, she encounters obstacles that test her resolve and strength. The first sign of trouble emerges when the vibrant colors of the Eternal Garden begin to fade, and the flowers that once bloomed with vivacity start to wilt. This decline is not merely a natural occurrence; it is the manifestation of a deeper darkness that threatens to engulf her world. As she navigates her childhood, Jastyn is often met with skepticism from her peers, who doubt her dreams of becoming a guardian of the blooms. Their mockery serves as an emotional trial, planting seeds of self-doubt within her, forcing Jastyn to confront the very essence of her purpose.

As Jastyn grows older, she faces increasingly formidable challenges. The Elders of the Eternal Garden, once distant figures of reverence, become pivotal in her journey. They reveal her connection to an ancient prophecy that binds her fate to the flowers she has always cherished. However, this newfound knowledge brings its own burdens. Jastyn grapples with the weight of expectation, feeling the pressure of her role as a protector. The Elders' cryptic warnings about the encroaching darkness serve as constant reminders of the stakes involved. Each encounter with them is a trial of both her understanding and her commitment to the sacred duty that awaits her.

In the heart of her trials lies the struggle against the creeping shadows that threaten the Eternal Garden. Jastyn embarks on a quest to discover the source of this darkness, a journey that tests her resilience and courage. Along the way, she faces various adversities, from treacherous landscapes to encounters with mythical creatures corrupted by despair. Each trial shapes her character, teaching her vital lessons about sacrifice and the importance of friendship. Jastyn learns that she cannot shoulder the burden alone; her strength lies in the bonds she forms with those who share her vision of restoring the garden's vitality. This realization marks a turning point in her journey, reinforcing the idea that unity is essential in overcoming the trials that lie ahead.

As Jastyn delves deeper into her quest, she uncovers hidden truths about her lineage and the history of the Eternal Garden. These revelations bring both clarity and confusion, as the past intertwines with her present. She discovers that the flowers she loves are not mere decorations of her world but living entities that resonate with the emotions of those who tend to them. This connection amplifies her sense of responsibility, and the weight of her destiny becomes heavier. Each flower she encounters tells a story, echoing the trials of those who came before her. Jastyn realizes that understanding these histories is crucial for her to fulfill her role in the unfolding prophecy.

Ultimately, Jastyn's trials and tribulations serve as a crucible for her transformation. Through every challenge, she emerges stronger and more aware of the profound impact she can have on her world. The darkness, once a daunting adversary, becomes a catalyst for her growth. Jastyn learns that her journey is not just about saving the flowers but also about embracing her identity as the Gift from God. Each trial she faces enriches her understanding of herself and her purpose, leading her closer to the moment when she will stand as the guardian of the Eternal Garden. In this intricate dance of light and shadow, Jastyn discovers that her true power lies not only in her destiny but in the choices she makes along the way.

THE PATH OF THE CHOSEN

The path of the chosen is often fraught with trials and revelations, and for Jastyn, this journey begins in the tranquil village of Eldergrove. Nestled at the edge of the Eternal Garden, Eldergrove thrives under the watchful eyes of the flowers that bloom vibrantly with each passing season. These flowers are more than mere decorations; they are the essence of life in Jastyn's world, embodying the memories and wisdom of the ancients. Unbeknownst to her, Jastyn carries within her the legacy of a long-forgotten prophecy, a destiny that intertwines her fate with the very fabric of the realm's existence.

As she matures, Jastyn finds herself drawn to the more secluded areas of the Eternal Garden, where the blooms whisper secrets only she can hear. The Elders, guardians of the garden's ancient knowledge, observe her with both hope and concern. They recognize a glimmer of the extraordinary within her, yet she remains oblivious to the weight of her heritage. The connection between Jastyn and the flora deepens, revealing glimpses of her potential to harness their power. This bond is a reflection of her pure heart, a quality that the Elders deem essential for the one destined to restore balance to their world.

The tranquility of Eldergrove is shattered when a creeping darkness begins to invade the sacred lands. The flowers, once vibrant and full of life, begin to wilt, their colors dimming as their life force is siphoned away. Jastyn witnesses her beloved blooms fading, and an unsettling sense of urgency ignites within her. The Elders, sensing the encroaching threat, initiate a series of rituals to protect the garden, but their efforts are only a temporary reprieve. It is in this moment of despair that Jastyn stumbles upon a hidden chamber within the garden, where she discovers the truth about her lineage and the prophecy that names her as the Gift from God.

Awakening to her destiny, Jastyn understands that she must embrace her role as the chosen one. The knowledge she gains from the Elders equips her with the skills to channel the power of the flowers, but it also places a heavy burden on her shoulders. The path ahead is unclear and filled with challenges, yet her resolve strengthens. Jastyn learns that the true essence of being chosen is not merely about the power she wields, but about the choices she makes and the compassion she extends to others. Each step she takes is guided by the memories held within the blooms, connecting her to the countless souls who have walked this path before her.

As Jastyn sets forth on her quest to confront the encroaching darkness, she realizes that the journey is as significant as the destination. Along the way, she encounters allies who join her cause, each with their own connection to the Eternal Garden. Together, they navigate treacherous landscapes and unravel the mysteries of the prophecy that binds them. Jastyn's path as the chosen one becomes a testament to the strength of unity and the power of love that transcends the darkness threatening their world. In embracing her identity, Jastyn not only seeks to restore the blooms but also to fulfill the promise of a brighter future for all creatures who call the mystical realm home.

CHAPTER SIX

FACING THE UNKNOWN

THE SECRETS OF THE NIGHT

The night in the realm of Jastyn is not merely a time when the sun retreats; it is a canvas painted with the secrets of the universe. As twilight descends, the flowers awaken, their petals unfurling to reveal luminous patterns that shimmer under the moonlight. Each bloom, a vessel of ancient power, begins to pulse with energy, revealing the hidden wisdom accumulated over centuries. The Elders of the Eternal Garden often spoke of these nocturnal revelations, emphasizing that the true magic of the flowers is unveiled only when the stars align and the world quiets down. It is during these hours of darkness that Jastyn would begin her journey of discovery, unraveling the mysteries that lie beneath the surface.

In the heart of the Eternal Garden, whispers of the night dance among the petals, carrying tales of those who came before. These stories are not just remnants of the past but living memories that connect the present to a lineage of guardians. Each flower, from the radiant Night Bloom to the ethereal Moonshade, holds fragments of knowledge, waiting for a pure-hearted soul to unlock their potential. Jastyn, though initially unaware of her significance, becomes instinctively drawn to these blooms, sensing an unexplainable bond that ties her to the secrets they harbor. The night acts as a bridge, allowing her to tap into the wisdom of the ages, guiding her toward her destiny.

As darkness envelops the realm, it also brings forth the shadows that threaten the very essence of the Eternal Garden. The encroaching gloom is a manifestation of despair, sapping the life force from the flowers and dimming their once-vibrant colors. Jastyn feels the weight of this darkness, recognizing that it is not merely a physical phenomenon but a reflection of the turmoil within the hearts of the people. The Elders had taught that light and dark exist in a delicate balance, and it is within this balance that Jastyn finds her purpose. The secrets of the night reveal to her that she must become a beacon of hope, harnessing the power of the blooms to combat the spreading shadow.

Through her nocturnal explorations, Jastyn begins to uncover the ancient prophecies inscribed within the petals. These prophecies speak of a chosen one who would rise to restore harmony, a role that she discovers is intertwined with her very identity. Each night, as she listens to the flowers, she learns of the trials and tribulations that await her. The blooms share their strength, and in return, Jastyn vows to protect them from the looming threat. The revelations of the night not only empower her but also instill a profound understanding of her connection to the garden and its inhabitants, solidifying her place in the tapestry of fate.

Ultimately, "The Secrets of the Night" serves as a pivotal chapter in Jastyn's journey, illustrating the intricate relationship between darkness and light. It is within the quiet moments of the night that clarity emerges, allowing Jastyn to embrace her role as the Gift of the Eternal Bloom. The flowers, once mere objects of beauty, become allies in her quest, their secrets guiding her steps as she strives to reclaim the light. As the world awakens each dawn, Jastyn stands ready to face the challenges ahead, her heart blooming with newfound purpose, forever changed by the revelations of the night.

A TEST OF COURAGE

As Jastyn ventured deeper into the heart of the Eternal Garden, she felt a palpable shift in the air. The vibrant hues of the flowers that once surrounded her now dulled, their petals wilting as shadows encroached upon their beauty. This transformation was not merely a reflection of the garden's state but a signal of the growing darkness threatening to consume her home. Jastyn understood that her journey was not just about discovering her identity; it was about confronting the fears that gripped her heart and threatened the very essence of the world she cherished.

The Elders of the Eternal Garden had entrusted Jastyn with a monumental task: to restore the balance between light and darkness. However, to fulfill her destiny, she needed to harness the courage that lay dormant within her. As she stood before the ancient Tree of Wisdom, its branches heavy with the weight of untold knowledge, she felt the pressure of her lineage and the expectations placed upon her. In that moment, Jastyn was reminded of the stories her grandmother told her, tales of brave souls who overcame insurmountable odds. It was time for her to embody the spirit of those legends.

With a resolute heart, Jastyn decided to seek out the source of the darkness. She recalled the whispers of the garden, the way the flowers had once guided her steps. Their songs of hope echoed in her mind, urging her to push forward despite her trepidation. Armed with the knowledge from the Elders and the memories of her ancestors, she journeyed into the shadowed depths of the realm, where the light of the Eternal Garden began to fade. Each step felt heavier than the last, yet each breath filled her with a growing determination.

As she approached the heart of the darkness, Jastyn encountered manifestations of her fears: illusions that taunted her with self-doubt and despair. The specters of inadequacy loomed large, whispering that she was not worthy of the gift she carried. Yet in the face of these trials, she began to recognize the strength within her. With each challenge overcome, she felt a surge of power that resonated with the blooms she had come to protect. The flowers, vibrant in their resilience, became her allies, offering their strength as she confronted the shadows threatening to engulf her.

In that climactic moment, standing at the crossroads of fear and courage, Jastyn realized that her true strength lay not in her ability to banish darkness alone but in her connection to the garden and its eternal blooms. She summoned the memories of joy, love, and unity that the flowers represented, channeling them into a radiant light that surged forth to combat the shadows. In that test of courage, she discovered that embracing her vulnerabilities was just as powerful as wielding her gifts. With newfound clarity, Jastyn took her place as the guardian of the Eternal Garden, ready to reclaim the light and restore the balance of life.

THE HEART OF A BLOOM

In the mystical realm of Jastyn, flowers transcend their natural existence, embodying the essence of life, history, and magic. Each bloom serves as a vessel, intricately woven with the stories of those who have tended to the land, representing a lineage that connects the past, present, and future. The petals of a single flower can whisper secrets of ancient times, while the roots intertwine with the very heartbeat of the earth. This connection between the flora and the inhabitants of the realm is vital, as it reflects the balance of nature and the purity of intention that sustains the life force of the Eternal Garden.

As Jastyn navigates her childhood, she remains blissfully ignorant of her significance within this intricate tapestry of life. Raised in a small village, she finds joy in the vibrant colors and fragrant scents that surround her, often playing among the blooms without understanding their deeper meanings. The elders of her community teach her to respect the flowers, but they hold back the truth of her destiny. Unbeknownst to her, Jastyn possesses a purity of heart that resonates with the essence of the Eternal Garden, marking her as a chosen protector. This role is not merely a title but a calling that will soon unveil the importance of her connection to the realm's lifeblood.

The emergence of darkness represents a pivotal moment in the story of Jastyn and her world. As shadows creep into the vibrant landscape, the flowers begin to wither, their vitality stolen by an unseen force. This encroaching malevolence serves to highlight the fragility of the balance that Jastyn and her people have taken for granted. The once-thriving flora, which served as a source of nourishment and inspiration, now stands as a testament to the peril that threatens to consume the very essence of life in the realm. It is through this darkness that Jastyn's journey of self-discovery begins, pushing her to seek answers and confront her identity.

The revelation of Jastyn's name—a name steeped in forgotten prophecy—unlocks the potential that lies dormant within her. As she learns about the Elders and the significance of the Eternal Garden, her purpose becomes clearer. This awakening is not just about individual power; it is a call to rally the spirits of the flowers and the people who inhabit her realm. Jastyn must embrace her role as the Gift from God, a beacon of hope amidst despair, and harness the ancient wisdom that the blooms have to offer. The power of a bloom is not solely in its beauty but in its ability to inspire courage and unity in the face of adversity.

Ultimately, the heart of a bloom symbolizes resilience and regeneration. It is through the trials and tribulations that Jastyn will learn to harness her inner strength and invoke the hidden magic of the Eternal Garden. As she confronts the darkness threatening her world, she will uncover the interconnectedness of all living beings and the importance of nurturing the bonds that tie them together. The journey ahead will challenge her, but it will also illuminate the path to restoring harmony and ensuring that the stories contained within each bloom continue to flourish for generations to come.

CHAPTER SEVEN

THE HEART OF THE GARDEN

THE SACRED BLOOM

In the heart of the mystical realm where Jastyn resides, flowers are revered not merely for their beauty but as embodiments of ancient power and wisdom. Each bloom serves as a vessel, carrying stories of love, hope, and the very essence of life itself. The vibrant colors and intoxicating scents are not accidental; they are manifestations of the energies that flow through the Eternal Garden. This sacred land, accessible only to those deemed worthy by the Elders, pulses with the heartbeat of nature, reminding all who enter of the delicate balance that sustains their world.

As Jastyn grows, she remains blissfully unaware of her unique connection to this enchanted flora. Her childhood is filled with joyous explorations among the petals and vines, where she feels an inexplicable bond with the blooms that surround her. The Elders, custodians of the Eternal Garden, watch over her from afar, knowing that she embodies a destiny intertwined with the very fabric of their existence. The whispers of the flowers tell tales of an impending darkness, a threat that looms ever closer, but for Jastyn, these omens are mere shadows dancing at the edges of her consciousness.

The tranquility of Jastyn's life begins to unravel as the darkness encroaches, siphoning the vitality from the sacred flowers. The once-vibrant garden starts to wither, sending ripples of despair through the realm. Jastyn, feeling an unexplainable ache in her heart, is drawn to the Elders, seeking answers to the turmoil unfolding around her. It is in their presence that she learns of her true identity and the prophecy that has been etched into the annals of time. Her name, Jastyn, signifies a beacon of hope, destined to restore the lost life force to the garden and banish the encroaching shadows.

With the revelation of her purpose, Jastyn embarks on a journey to reclaim the sacred blooms that have begun to fade. Each flower she encounters reveals its own story, a fragment of the collective memory that binds their world together. As she learns to communicate with the flora, Jastyn discovers the power of compassion and understanding, realizing that the key to restoring the garden lies not just in her actions but in the connections she forges with the natural world. The vibrant petals, once mere decorations of her childhood, now become allies in her quest, each bloom lending its strength and wisdom to her burgeoning abilities.

In her pursuit to heal the Eternal Garden, Jastyn embraces her role as the Gift from God, an embodiment of the sacred bloom that symbolizes renewal and hope. As she confronts the darkness that threatens to engulf her realm, she learns that the true essence of the sacred bloom extends beyond its physical presence; it is a testament to resilience, unity, and the unwavering spirit of life. Through her journey, Jastyn not only seeks to restore the flowers but also uncovers her place within the tapestry of a world that flourishes when nurtured by love, understanding, and the eternal cycle of rebirth.

THE CONNECTION TO NATURE

In the mystical realm of Jastyn, nature serves as a living tapestry, intricately woven with the stories of the past and the whispers of the future. Each flower, vibrant and unique, is imbued with the essence of ancient power, acting as a bridge between the physical world and the spiritual realm. This deep-rooted connection to nature not only defines the landscape but also shapes the identity of its inhabitants. The Elders of the Eternal Garden, guardians of this sacred place, recognize the profound relationship between the flowers and the well-being of all living beings, emphasizing that harmony with nature is essential for prosperity.

As Jastyn grows, she remains blissfully unaware of the sacred significance of her surroundings. The lush meadows and towering trees are more than mere scenery; they are alive with energy and purpose. The flowers not only provide beauty but also convey messages from the past, chronicling the lives of those who came before. Each petal holds a story, each fragrance carries a memory, and each bloom serves a unique function in the ecosystem. This interconnectedness is foundational to Jastyn's identity, as she is destined to play a pivotal role in maintaining the balance of this enchanting realm.

The arrival of darkness, however, threatens to unravel the delicate fabric of this connection. As the life force of the sacred flowers begins to diminish, Jastyn witnesses firsthand the devastating impact on her world. The once-vibrant colors fade, and the melodic hum of nature grows silent. This decline serves as a stark reminder of the intrinsic bond between the health of the flowers and the vitality of the realm itself. Jastyn's journey becomes not only a quest to restore the beauty of her surroundings but also a deeper exploration of her own identity and purpose as a protector of nature.

In her quest to understand the true meaning of her name and the forgotten prophecy, Jastyn discovers the wisdom of the Elders. They teach her that the key to revitalizing the land lies in nurturing the connection between humanity and nature. By fostering this bond, she learns to harness the power of the blooms, using their energy to heal and restore. This understanding transcends mere survival; it becomes a spiritual awakening that aligns her with the rhythms of the earth, fostering a sense of belonging and responsibility toward all living things.

Ultimately, Jastyn's journey reflects the broader theme of coexistence with nature. As she embraces her role as the Gift from God, she recognizes that the fate of the Eternal Garden is intertwined with her own. The flowers flourish when treated with respect and love, and in turn, they empower Jastyn to rise against the encroaching darkness. Through her connection to nature, she embodies the hope of renewal, illustrating that the strength of a single heart can indeed bloom into a force powerful enough to restore balance to an entire realm.

HARNESSING THE ETERNAL POWER

In the mystical realm of Jastyn, flowers transcend their physical existence, embodying ancient wisdom and energy that pulses through the fabric of life itself. Each blossom serves as a repository of stories, memories, and the essence of existence, cultivated by the Elders of the Eternal Garden. These Elders, guardians of nature's balance, have long understood the significance of the flowers, recognizing them as vital conduits of power that connect the spirit of the earth with its inhabitants. Jastyn, born into this vibrant world, remains blissfully unaware of the immense potential she possesses, destined to become a beacon of hope amid encroaching darkness.

As Jastyn matures, her surroundings whisper to her, each petal and leaf resonating with the pulse of the ancient magic that permeates her homeland. It is in her interactions with the flora that she begins to feel an inexplicable connection, an intrinsic bond that hints at her greater purpose. The flowers seem to respond to her emotions, blooming more vibrantly in her presence, and yet, a shadow looms over the land as malevolent forces threaten to drain the life from these sacred plants. The darkening skies and wilting blossoms serve as ominous signs, foretelling a crisis that will soon demand Jastyn's awakening.

When Jastyn learns of her selection by the Elders, she discovers the weight of her destiny. The prophecy tied to her name reveals that she is not merely a guardian but a pivotal force in the battle against the darkness. As she delves deeper into her lineage, she realizes that the power of the Eternal Garden flows through her veins, granting her the ability to harness the very essence of the flowers. This revelation prompts a profound transformation within her, as Jastyn embraces the responsibility that comes with her gift. The time has come for her to rise, to cultivate not just the blooms but also her own strength.

To harness the eternal power effectively, Jastyn must first learn the intricate language of the flowers. Each species communicates its needs and desires, and through patience and intuition, she begins to understand their silent cries for help. Guided by the Elders, she practices rituals that draw upon the energy of the blossoms, channeling their vitality to restore what has been lost. With every successful invocation, she feels the connection between her spirit and the earth deepen, revealing the profound truth that she is an integral part of this cycle of life. Her journey becomes one of mutual nurturing, where the blooms empower her, and in turn, she revives their fading glow.

As the darkness encroaches further, Jastyn's mastery over the eternal power becomes crucial. The knowledge she acquires transforms her into a defender of the realm, capable of wielding the energy of the flowers to combat the shadow that seeks to consume their light. With each challenge she faces, her resolve strengthens, and she gathers allies who share her vision of restoring balance.

The path ahead is fraught with uncertainty, but Jastyn understands that the power of the Eternal Garden lies not only in its blooms but also in the unity of purpose among those who cherish the natural world. In harnessing this eternal power, she not only fulfills her destiny but ignites a movement that reverberates through the very heart of her enchanted realm.

CHAPTER EIGHT

CONFRONTING THE DARKNESS

THE BATTLE FOR THE BLOOMS

The battle for the blooms began as a fight not just for survival, but for the very essence of life that flowed through the mystical realm of Jastyn. Each flower in this enchanted land was imbued with ancient powers, representing the memories and stories of those who had come before. The Elders of the Eternal Garden, guardians of this sacred space, had long ensured that the balance between light and darkness was maintained. However, as shadows from the outside world began to encroach upon their realm, the vibrant colors of the flowers started to fade, and a sense of urgency enveloped Jastyn and her companions.

As Jastyn learned of her connection to the blooms, she began to understand the gravity of the situation. The darkness was not merely a physical entity but a manifestation of despair and greed that threatened to consume the purity of the flowers. Each bloom that lost its vitality weakened the bonds of the realm, leading to chaos and imbalance. With the Elders' guidance, Jastyn realized that she had a pivotal role to play in this impending battle, as her very existence was intertwined with the fate of the flowers. The prophecy that had long been forgotten now echoed in her mind, urging her to embrace her destiny.

The first confrontation came at the edge of the Eternal Garden, where the darkness had begun to seep through the barriers that protected the blooms. Jastyn and her allies, a diverse group of guardians from various corners of their world, prepared to face the encroaching shadows. They wielded not only their physical strength but also the deep-rooted knowledge of the blooms' powers. Each guardian had a unique affinity with a specific flower, enhancing their abilities in the fight. Jastyn, linked to the rarest bloom, a radiant flower said to hold the essence of hope, felt a surge of energy as she stepped forward to lead the charge.

The battle unfolded with vibrant colors clashing against the dark void. As the guardians fought valiantly, Jastyn began to unlock the full potential of her connection to the sacred blooms. She summoned the energies of the flowers, weaving them into a protective barrier that shielded her allies from the darkness's corrupting touch. With each bloom that she nurtured, she could feel the life force strengthening, pushing back against the encroaching shadows. However, the darkness was relentless, and Jastyn soon realized that this battle was not just a physical struggle but also a test of her inner strength and conviction.

As the battle raged on, the true meaning of the blooms became clear to Jastyn. They were not merely tools of power; they were symbols of unity, resilience, and the interconnectedness of all life. With this realization, she rallied her companions, reminding them of the stories and memories each bloom held. Together, they fought not just for the flowers but for the very essence of their world. In that moment, Jastyn understood that the battle for the blooms was a battle for hope itself, and as they pushed back the shadows, she felt the blooms responding, their vibrant colors shining brighter than ever, heralding a new dawn for Jastyn and her realm.

JASTYN'S TRANSFORMATION

Jastyn's journey of transformation begins in the lush, vibrant landscapes of the Eternal Garden, a realm teeming with life and energy. As a child, she perceives the flowers around her as mere companions, unaware of the profound significance embedded in their existence. Each bloom, with its vibrant colors and intoxicating scents, whispers stories of the past, yet Jastyn remains oblivious to her connection to this mystical world. Her playful innocence allows her to dance through fields of blossoms, marveling at their beauty, but it is only the first layer of her destiny that she experiences.

As Jastyn matures, subtle shifts in her surroundings become apparent. The once-bustling garden begins to dim, and the flowers lose their luster. It is during these troubling times that Jastyn encounters the Elders of the Eternal Garden, wise beings who have watched over the realm for centuries. They reveal to her the gravity of the situation: darkness is encroaching, threatening to extinguish the life force of the sacred flowers. This revelation marks a pivotal moment in her life, igniting a spark of awareness within her. She learns that her name, Jastyn, is not just a label but a key to an ancient prophecy, one that foretells her role as a beacon of hope and renewal.

Awakened to her purpose, Jastyn embarks on a profound journey of self-discovery. She begins to cultivate a deeper understanding of the flowers, learning to listen to their stories and harness their energies. Each interaction with the blooms reveals unique powers and wisdom, allowing her to form a bond that transcends the physical realm. Through meditation and introspection, she discovers her own innate abilities, realizing that she is not merely a caretaker of the garden but a vital force capable of restoring balance and harmony.

As Jastyn delves deeper into her transformation, she encounters trials that test her resolve. The darkness that threatens the Eternal Garden manifests in various forms, challenging her newfound powers and forcing her to confront her fears. With each obstacle, she grows stronger, her determination fueled by the love she feels for the flowers and the realm they inhabit. The experiences shape her into a resilient warrior, one who learns the importance of unity and compassion in the face of adversity. Her connection with the Elders deepens, and they guide her in mastering the sacred arts of restoration.

Ultimately, Jastyn's transformation culminates in a powerful realization: she is an integral thread in the tapestry of the Eternal Garden. As she embraces her role as the Gift from God, she stands poised to confront the encroaching darkness. Empowered by the wisdom of the Elders and the strength of the flowers, Jastyn embodies the spirit of the Eternal Bloom. Her journey not only signifies her personal evolution but also serves as a reminder of the resilience inherent in nature and the profound impact one individual can have in nurturing the world around them.

THE FINAL SHOWDOWN

The final showdown unfolds in the heart of the Eternal Garden, a place once vibrant with the colors and fragrances of countless flowers, now shrouded in shadows. Jastyn, having embraced her destiny, stands at the edge of the Garden, prepared to confront the darkness that threatens to consume it. The Elders, guardians of the realm, gather in a circle, their ancient eyes reflecting both wisdom and worry. They recount the tales of the darkness, a force born from despair and greed, which has long sought to extinguish the light of the blooms. Jastyn learns that in order to restore balance, she must tap into the power of her lineage and the gifts bestowed upon her by the sacred flowers.

As Jastyn walks deeper into the Garden, she feels the weight of the prophecy resting on her shoulders. Each step resonates with the whispers of the blooms, urging her to remember the stories they hold within. She reaches the heart of the Garden, where the oldest flower, the Lumina Blossom, stands wilting under the pressure of the encroaching darkness. This flower, revered by the Elders, symbolizes hope and renewal. Jastyn understands that to save the Lumina Blossom is to save her world. Drawing upon her connection with the flowers, she begins to channel their energy, feeling the warmth of their life force flow through her, igniting a spark of determination within.

The air thickens as the darkness takes form, a swirling mass of despair and malice that seeks to extinguish the light of the blooms. Jastyn faces the embodiment of this darkness, a shadowy figure who laughs mockingly at her courage. The figure taunts her, revealing the depths of her fears and the fragility of her resolve. However, fueled by the memories and hopes of the countless blooms, Jastyn stands firm. She recalls the teachings of the Elders, the lessons of compassion, resilience, and unity. With each memory, she feels her connection to the flowers strengthen, transforming her fear into a powerful force of light.

The final confrontation erupts in a dazzling display of colors and shadows, as Jastyn unleashes the energy of the Eternal Garden. The flowers respond to her call, their petals unfurling in a symphony of vibrant hues that clash against the darkness. With each pulse of energy, Jastyn weaves a tapestry of light, creating a barrier that pushes back against the encroaching shadows. The Lumina Blossom, rejuvenated by her efforts, emits a brilliant glow, amplifying Jastyn's power. Together, they become a beacon of hope, illuminating the Garden and inspiring the other flowers to join the fight against the darkness.

As the battle reaches its climax, Jastyn channels the full force of her heritage, embodying the spirit of the blooms and the will of the Elders. In a final surge of energy, she confronts the shadowy figure, declaring that the light of the Eternal Garden will never be extinguished. With a blinding flash, the darkness dissipates, leaving behind only the faint echoes of its malevolence. The Garden, once again, flourishes with life, the flowers blooming brighter than ever. Jastyn stands victorious, not only as a savior but as a symbol of hope, embodying the essence of the prophecy. The final showdown marks not just the end of darkness but the beginning of a new era for the Eternal Garden, one where Jastyn's legacy and the power of the blooms will forever thrive.

CHAPTER NINE

THE RESTORATION

HEALING THE GARDEN

In the heart of the Eternal Garden, healing was not merely a matter of tending to the soil or nurturing the blooms. It was a profound connection between the caretaker and the essence of life itself. Jastyn, with her innate bond to the garden, began to understand that each flower held a fragment of the universe's memory, a testament to the harmony that once flourished in this sacred space. The vibrant colors and intoxicating scents masked a deeper truth —one that spoke of imbalance and the encroaching shadows that threatened to extinguish the garden's magic. As Jastyn embarked on her journey of healing, she learned that restoring the garden meant rekindling the lost stories of the flowers.

The Elders of the Eternal Garden had long known that the vitality of the blooms depended on the purity of intention and the strength of the heart. Jastyn's connection to the garden was unique; she could hear the whispers of the flowers, feel the pulse of the earth beneath her feet, and sense the sorrow that permeated the air. Each petal that wilted and each stem that drooped communicated a tale of despair, be it from forgotten dreams or unfulfilled promises. Jastyn realized that to heal the garden, she must first listen and understand the grievances of the blooms, for they were reflections of the world around her.

As darkness spread its tendrils, suffocating the essence of life, Jastyn sought out the ancient wisdom of the Elders. They revealed the rituals of restoration, which required more than just physical labor; they called for emotional and spiritual alignment with the garden's energies. Jastyn learned to harness the power of her emotions, channeling love, hope, and determination into her tending. This new approach transformed her actions from simple gardening tasks to sacred rituals that invoked the very spirit of the Eternal Garden. With each act of kindness, she breathed new life into the wilting flowers, coaxing them back from the brink of despair.

The journey of healing was not without its challenges. Jastyn faced moments of doubt and despair as she witnessed the relentless advance of darkness. However, these trials only deepened her resolve. She discovered that the garden was a reflection of her own growth; as she nurtured the flowers, she also nurtured her spirit. The blooms responded to her unwavering faith, slowly regaining their vibrancy as they shared their stories of resilience with her. Jastyn understood that healing the garden was a symbiotic relationship, one that required patience and trust in the natural cycle of life.

With time, the garden began to flourish once more, blossoming into a kaleidoscope of colors that danced in the sunlight. Jastyn's heart swelled with pride as she witnessed the transformation, knowing that she had played a crucial role in restoring balance to this sacred ground. The flowers sang their gratitude, and the winds carried their stories far and wide, spreading hope to the corners of the mystical realm. In this healing journey, Jastyn not only saved the garden but also discovered her own purpose as a guardian of the Eternal Bloom, destined to protect the delicate balance between light and shadow for generations to come.

THE RETURN OF LIGHT

The Return of Light marks a pivotal moment in Jastyn's journey, representing not just a physical restoration but a resurgence of hope and vitality within her mystical realm. As darkness looms, the once-vibrant flowers of the Eternal Garden begin to wither, their colors fading under the weight of despair. Each petal that falls is a symbol of lost memories and diminished purpose, echoing the sorrow of a world that thrived on the beauty and power of its blossoms.

Jastyn, initially unaware of her connection to this sacred place, feels a stirring within her spirit, an awakening that compels her to seek the truth behind her identity and the fate of the flowers.

In her quest, Jastyn encounters the Elders of the Eternal Garden, wise beings who reveal her destiny as the chosen one. They share the ancient prophecy tied to her name, illustrating how she embodies the spirit of renewal and transformation. The Elders explain that her presence is integral to restoring balance and that she must harness the energy of the blooms, which are intricately linked to the life force of the realm. With each revelation, Jastyn's understanding deepens, and she begins to comprehend the magnitude of her gift and the responsibility it entails. The prophecy speaks of a time when the darkness will be confronted, and the light will return, symbolizing the triumph of hope over despair.

As Jastyn steps into her role, she learns to communicate with the flora around her. Each flower reveals its unique story, offering her insights into the history of the realm and the nature of the darkness encroaching upon it. This connection not only strengthens her resolve but also imbues her with the ability to summon the latent power of the blooms. Through her bond with the flowers, she discovers that the light is not merely a force to overcome darkness; it is a living essence that flows through all beings, reminding her that every creature has a part to play in the grand tapestry of existence.

The journey to restore the light becomes increasingly perilous as Jastyn faces adversaries drawn to the fading energy of the Eternal Garden. These entities thrive on despair, seeking to extinguish the last remnants of hope. Yet, with each confrontation, Jastyn learns to harness her growing power, drawing strength from the stories and memories embedded within the flowers. The battles she faces are not just external but also internal, as she grapples with her fears and doubts. Each victory, however small, serves to illuminate her path, reinforcing her belief in the prophecy and the promise of renewal.

Ultimately, The Return of Light signifies a transformation not only for Jastyn but for the entire realm. As she embraces her identity and purpose, the flowers begin to bloom anew, vibrant colors spilling forth as if the very essence of life is being restored. The darkness that once threatened to engulf the Eternal Garden recedes, replaced by the warmth of hope and the brilliance of unity. Jastyn's journey becomes a testament to the power of belief, resilience, and the profound connection between all living things, reminding readers that even in the darkest times, the light is never truly lost; it awaits the moment to return.

THE NEW ERA OF BLOOMS

The New Era of Blooms marks a pivotal transition in the realm of Jastyn, where the harmony between nature and magic begins to unravel. For centuries, the flowers of the Eternal Garden thrived, sustaining the delicate balance of life and magic within the realm. Each bloom, vibrant and alive, served as a keeper of the past, holding within its petals the tales of those who came before. The Elders, wise guardians of this sacred land, recognized the profound connection between the flowers and the inhabitants of Jastyn, ensuring that the secrets of the blooms remained protected and cherished.

As the darkness encroaches upon this once-luminous world, the Elders sense the shift. The vibrant hues of the flowers begin to fade, and the melodies of the garden grow silent. The life force that nourished the blooms is siphoned away, leaving behind a hushed desolation. In this new era, the flowers that once brought joy and vitality are transformed into symbols of a looming crisis. Jastyn, still unaware of her destiny, feels the weight of this change in her heart, sensing a call to action that resonates deep within her soul.

Jastyn's journey toward understanding her unique role in this unfolding drama begins as she uncovers her connection to the Eternal Garden. The realization that she is chosen by the Elders ignites a spark of courage within her. She learns that her name is intertwined with an ancient prophecy, one that speaks of a hero who will restore the balance between light and darkness. This revelation propels her into a world of challenges and discoveries, where the fate of both the flowers and her own existence hangs in the balance.

As Jastyn embarks on her quest, she encounters allies and adversaries alike, each with their own ties to the blooms. The characters she meets reveal the multifaceted nature of the realm, illustrating how deeply intertwined the lives of the flowers and their caretakers truly are. Through their stories, Jastyn gains insight into the history of the Eternal Garden, learning that every petal and leaf carries the essence of life's experiences. This knowledge empowers her, fueling her determination to fight against the encroaching darkness.

In The New Era of Blooms, Jastyn's journey is not just about saving the flowers; it is a quest for identity, purpose, and the reclamation of hope. As she embraces her role as the Gift from God, she comes to understand that the true power of the blooms lies not merely in their beauty but in their ability to connect, heal, and inspire. This new era heralds not just a battle against darkness, but the awakening of an inner strength that will lead to the restoration of the Eternal Garden, ensuring that the luminous legacy of the blooms will continue to thrive for generations to come.

CHAPTER TEN

THE LEGACY OF JASTYN

THE IMPACT ON THE REALM

The impact of Jastyn's arrival in the mystical realm reverberates through every corner of the Eternal Garden. The Elders, who have long safeguarded the balance of nature and magic, sense a shift the moment she steps into their hallowed grounds. Her presence reignites the dwindling energy of the flowers, which have begun to wilt under the shadow of encroaching darkness. Each petal pulsates with renewed vigor, and the vibrant colors that once defined the landscape begin to reemerge. This transformation not only affects the flora but also the fauna that call this land home, as creatures who had retreated in fear start to venture forth, drawn by the revitalizing aura Jastyn embodies.

Jastyn's innate connection to the blooms unveils the profound relationship between the inhabitants of the realm and the flowers that surround them. Each bloom serves as a testament to the histories and experiences of the realm's denizens, encapsulating their joys, sorrows, and dreams. As Jastyn interacts with these flowers, she discovers their hidden stories, unlocking forgotten wisdom that had been lost to time. This process cultivates a deeper understanding among the people of Jastyn's world, fostering a revival of ancient traditions that honor the bonds between nature and the beings that inhabit it.

The darkness that threatens the realm does not merely act as a backdrop; it shapes the actions and decisions of its inhabitants. As the life force of the flowers dwindles, the community grapples with fear and uncertainty. Some factions may seek power through control of the remaining resources, while others rally around Jastyn, recognizing her as a beacon of hope. This division creates a complex social landscape, compelling Jastyn to navigate alliances and rivalries. Her journey becomes a microcosm of the larger struggle between light and dark, highlighting the importance of unity and collective purpose in overcoming adversity.

Moreover, Jastyn's emergence as a central figure in the realm catalyzes a re-examination of the Elders' role. Once seen as mere guardians, they are now mentors and guides who must adapt to the evolving dynamics introduced by Jastyn. Their teachings, once steeped in tradition, must now incorporate the fresh perspective that Jastyn brings. This evolution in mentorship reflects the necessity of adapting wisdom to meet contemporary challenges, emphasizing that the past must inform the future while remaining flexible to change.

Ultimately, the impact on the realm is profound, extending beyond the immediate threat posed by darkness. Jastyn's journey embodies the potential for renewal and transformation, not only within herself but also within the entire community. As she learns to harness the power of the blooms, she simultaneously inspires others to reconnect with their roots and reimagine their destinies. The realm of Jastyn, once threatened by despair, begins to flourish anew, illustrating that hope can thrive even in the direst of circumstances, and that the eternal bloom of life is always within reach for those willing to embrace their destiny.

A NEW GUARDIAN

In the heart of the Eternal Garden, a new chapter began with the emergence of Jastyn, a young girl whose laughter resonated like the soft rustle of petals in the breeze. The Elders of the Garden had long awaited her arrival, for she was destined to become the Guardian of the blooms. The significance of her name, once a mere whisper among the flowers, transformed into a powerful echo of ancient prophecies. Jastyn was not merely a child of the realm; she was the chosen one, imbued with the essence of life itself, entrusted with the sacred duty to protect the vibrant tapestry of flora that held the balance of their mystical world.

As she roamed the Garden, surrounded by blossoms that shimmered with colors unseen in other realms, Jastyn began to sense a profound connection to the flowers. Each petal, each stem, seemed to resonate with her spirit, sharing stories of joy and sorrow, hope and despair. The Elders, wise and gentle, guided her through the intricacies of their world, teaching her the language of the blooms. They spoke of the delicate interplay between light and shadow, the necessity of nurturing the blooms while remaining vigilant against the encroaching darkness threatening to consume their essence. Jastyn's heart swelled with purpose, yet uncertainty loomed as she grappled with the weight of her destined role.

The tranquility of the Garden shattered when ominous signs appeared. Flowers began to wilt, their vibrant colors fading into dull hues as if the very life force was being siphoned away. The Elders gathered, their brows furrowed in concern, as they sensed the dark energies infiltrating their sacred space. Jastyn watched, a mix of fear and determination igniting within her. She realized that the fate of the Garden rested upon her shoulders. The ancient prophecies spoke not only of a Guardian but of a warrior who would rise against the encroaching shadows, harnessing the strength of the blooms to restore harmony.

In her quest to understand her newfound role, Jastyn sought guidance from the spirits of the flowers, each possessing unique wisdom and gifts. They whispered secrets of resilience, teaching her how to channel their energy into powerful spells capable of pushing back the darkness. With each lesson, Jastyn grew more attuned to the rhythms of nature, learning to summon the strength of the blooms and weave it into her very being. She discovered that the love for her world was the strongest magic of all, empowering her to confront the malevolent forces that threatened to unravel the fabric of their existence.

Armed with the knowledge bestowed upon her by the Elders and the flowers, Jastyn began to embrace her identity as the new Guardian. Her heart, once filled with doubt, now radiated with the light of hope, illuminating the path ahead. As she prepared to face the impending darkness, she understood that her journey was not just about protecting the Garden but also about awakening the courage within herself and her fellow beings. The bloom of her destiny was just beginning, and with each step, she would weave her own story into the eternal tapestry of life, ensuring that the sacred blooms would continue to flourish for generations to come.

THE ETERNAL BLOOM LIVES ON

In the mystical realm of Jastyn, the essence of life is intricately woven into the vibrant tapestry of its flora. Each flower, whether it be a delicate petal or a robust bloom, serves as a vessel for ancient powers that have been cultivated over centuries. They are not mere decorations of nature; they possess memories of the past and the hopes for the future. This unique connection between the flowers and the realm's inhabitants fosters a deep respect for nature, as it is believed that every petal carries within it the whispers of the Elders of the Eternal Garden, guiding and nurturing the balance of life.

As Jastyn grows, she remains blissfully unaware of her significant role in this enchanted world. The Elders, guardians of the Eternal Garden, have chosen her for a purpose that transcends generations. Her laughter, innocence, and unwavering kindness resonate with the spirit of the flowers, making her a beacon of hope. However, the shadows of impending darkness loom on the horizon, threatening to disrupt the harmony that has existed for ages. This darkness is not merely a physical presence but a manifestation of despair and neglect, seeking to drain the life force from the sacred flowers entrusted to Jastyn's realm.

The turning point in Jastyn's journey occurs when she discovers the truth behind her name—a name steeped in a forgotten prophecy. This revelation ignites a spark within her, awakening an instinctive understanding of her connection to the Eternal Bloom. Each flower she encounters begins to reveal its story, forming a bond that empowers her to combat the encroaching darkness. The prophecy whispers the promise of restoration, urging her to harness the gifts bestowed upon her by the Elders. Jastyn realizes that she is not just a passive observer in this mystical land; she is an active participant in the battle for its survival.

As the darkness spreads, the vibrant colors of the flowers begin to fade, and the air thickens with a sense of impending doom. Jastyn feels the weight of the world pressing down on her shoulders, yet she draws strength from the very blooms that surround her. They become her allies, their resilience reflecting her own determination. Each step she takes toward the Eternal Garden reinforces her resolve to protect the sacred land, reminding her that the bond between the blooms and the people is a powerful force that cannot be easily severed.

In the face of adversity, the eternal bloom lives on, symbolizing hope, renewal, and the indomitable spirit of life. Jastyn's journey is a testament to the power of connection—between individuals, nature, and the ancient wisdom that flows through the realm. As she fights to restore the balance and revive the fading flowers, she embodies the very essence of the Eternal Bloom, reminding all that within every challenge lies the potential for growth and transformation. The story of Jastyn is not just her own; it is a reflection of the resilience inherent in all living things, a reminder that even in the darkest of times, the light of hope and the beauty of life will endure.

ALSO BY KENNETH HAINES

A TALE OF ESCAPE

A group of Earthlings, including a young woman named Elara, is abducted by an invisible alien ship to become part of a cosmic exhibition. Facing the reality of being observed by an alien audience, they form a bond and ignite a longing for freedom. Together, they plot their escape, daring to dream of returning to their lives on Earth. As they navigate their captivity and fight for autonomy, they are tested but remain unbroken, driven by the hope of weaving their experiences back into humanity's story.

WHISPERS IN THE SAND

Amidst the whispers of the sand and the caress of the Autumn sea, a tale of survival unfolds on the shores of a forsaken island. Here, young Selene and her father carve out an existence, relying on the embrace of nature and each other. Their bond, once threatened by tragedy, burgeons under the trials they face in this barren refuge. But when the island yields an unexpected reunion, the fabric of their family is woven together once more, painting a poignant portrait of hope and resilience. In the cool embrace of a late afternoon's breeze, Selene's heart finds solace, and together, they etch a new beginning upon their souls—an indelible whisper in the fabric of time.

TYLORIN

In the oppressive kingdom of Eldaf, where elves endure human cruelty, a desperate elf mother and her child find an unexpected ally in a compassionate human. Together, they embark on a perilous escape through secret paths and natural sanctuaries, aided by the whispers of the forest's denizens. Their journey leads them to an abandoned, tranquil cottage, where they begin a new life of resilience and love. United by courage and kinship, their bond transcends blood, offering hope and peace amidst the shadows of their past.

ECHOES OF LAUGHTER, ECHOES OF FEAR

In an abandoned amusement park reclaimed by nature, five young explorersâ€"three girls and two boysâ€" embark on an adventure filled with mystery and spectral intrigue. Amid peeling paint and rusting rides, they delve into the park's hidden sorrows, blending nostalgia with a sense of foreboding. As they confront both the park's secrets and their own fears, their journey becomes a test of courage, friendship, and the human spirit. In this eerie yet captivating odyssey, the line between joy and darkness blurs, leaving them to discover whether their bonds can light the way through the park's enigmatic shadows.

SEA OF SHADOWS

Stranded on a solitary island, young Helene navigates a journey of survival and self-discovery, guided by the wisdom of her late father and the lessons of the untamed wilderness. Amid the island's deceptive tranquility, she transforms grief into resilience, building a sanctuary from remnants of the past and forging a future shaped by love and fortitude. Through hardship, Helene finds strength in enduring connections, her father's

presence ever a guiding light. Her odyssey is one of emotional catharsis and renewal, where each dawn heralds the triumph of hope and the radiance of new beginnings.

Enchanted Citadel

In a realm where magic and technology intertwine, a group of elite space voyagers embarks on a perilous quest to recover the Chrono Crystal, an ancient gemstone vital for stabilizing the magical streams of their soaring sanctuary, the Enchanted Citadel. As they traverse vibrant yet conflicted planets, they face arcane guardians and looming threats of a malevolent siege. Amidst a cosmic battlefield where starships glide on waves of sorcery and science, the voyagers grapple with unity and betrayal, illuminating paths once hidden in the shadows.

Time has stopped

In *Time Has Stopped*, Elara and her band of weary travelers navigate an endless red desert, a harsh landscape that was once ruled by oceans and now conceals the secrets of a long-lost, water-bound civilization. Battling scorching heat, deceptive mirages, and unforgiving storms, their journey leads them to a colossal statue and an underground labyrinth echoing with the remnants of a forgotten world. Along the way, they form an unlikely bond with a mysterious creature whose loyalty may be their only hope for survival. As the desert tests their resilience and courage, each step comes with sacrifice, forcing them to confront how far they are willing to go to survive the relentless sands of time.

Starborn

In a distant cosmos, the crew of a valiant starship embarks on a perilous journey through the galactic veil, uncovering relics of the ancient Starborn civilization—artifacts of immense power and potential ruin. As they navigate celestial ruins and decipher esoteric transmissions, the explorers grapple with internal tensions and looming cosmic adversaries. Each discovery brings them closer to revolutionary breakthroughs while risking catastrophic consequences. Caught between enlightenment and oblivion, their odyssey becomes a profound reflection on the morality of progress and the price of knowledge, weaving a tale of human resolve amidst the vast, enigmatic expanse of the stars.

Tales of the Unknown

Word in the forest was that something wasn't right and the creatures were on edge and the slightest noise or movement made them run for cover. Word of this came to Sanction while he was foliage for food. A wagon rolled up and tossed a young girl child from it, she was wrapped inside a burlap potato bag and was tossed aside like trash. Child please dry them tears for you are safe in my forest, like I said no harm will come to you. She sits up and listens to his every word.

Jake found himself enjoying the solitude of the open road. That is, until his car started to sputter. A sudden jolt, leaving Jake stranded in the middle of nowhere. Desperate for help, Jake decided to head towards the building, hoping to find a phone or someone who could assist. Soon to find he has entered where time had stopped and the souls of who where left behind needed to be saved.

Whispers in the Sand

Amidst the whispers of the sand and the caress of the Autumn sea, a tale of survival unfolds on the shores of a forsaken island. Here, young Selene and her father carve out an existence, relying on the embrace of nature and each other. Their bond, once threatened by tragedy, burgeons under the trials they face in this barren refuge. But when the island yields an unexpected reunion, the fabric of their family is woven together once more, painting a poignant portrait of hope and resilience. In the cool embrace of a late afternoon's breeze, Selene's heart finds solace, and together, they etch a new beginning upon their souls—an indelible whisper in the fabric of time.